Copyright © 1993 by Editions Dessain.
First published in French as *Mon Chien, Ma Soeur et Moi*
by Editions Dessain, an imprint of De Boeck-Wesmael S. A.,
Avenue Louise, 203, 1050 Bruxelles.
English translation copyright © 1993 by Tambourine Books.

Library of Congress Cataloging in Publication Data

Strub, Susanne, [*Mon chien, ma soeur, et moi*. English]
My dog, my sister, and I/by Susanne Strub.—1st U.S. ed. p.cm.
Summary: A six-year-old boy compares his rate of growth with that
of his two-year-old sister and their two-year-old-dog.
[1. Growth—Fiction.   2. Brothers and sisters—Fiction. 3. Dogs—Fiction.]
I. Title. PZ7.S9258Myf   1993 [E]—dc20—92-22063   CIP   AC
ISBN 0-688-12010-5 (TR).—ISBN 0-688-12011-3   (LE)

10 9 8 7 6 5 4 3 2 1
First U.S. edition

Jerabek
Elementary
School

BIRTHDAY BOOK CLUB

donated by

LINDSEY TOWER

March 23, 1994

My Dog,
My Sister, and I

Susanne Strub

TAMBOURINE BOOKS

NEW YORK

In the beginning, there was only me.
I was a baby. I don't remember much,
but we have lots of photos.

Here I am at two.

I was still a baby.

By the time I was four, I was driving trains—
but only in my living room.

Then my little sister Annie came.
She didn't grow very fast either.

With Sparky, it was different.
He was also a baby when he arrived,
right after Annie was born.

He always cried at night and
we had to comfort him.

Just like Annie.

Sparky needed to go outside
a lot,

and he ate and ate and ate.

Annie stayed indoors,

and she drank and drank
and drank.

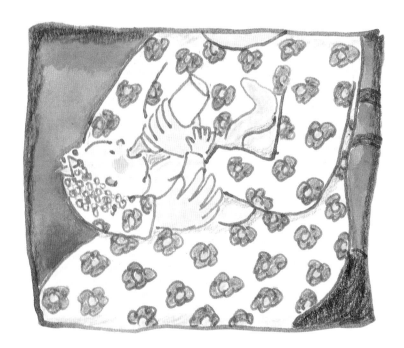

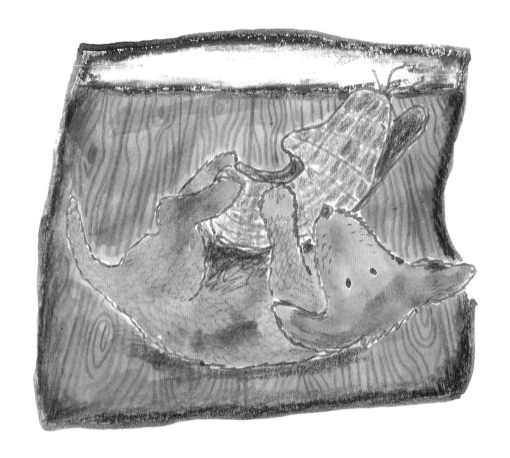

Sparky chewed on our slippers.

Annie sucked on her toes.

Soon Sparky could be fed just two times a day.

And he didn't cry every night.

It took longer for Annie.

Sparky hardly ever has accidents anymore.

Annie still needs diapers.

Sparky always finds toys by himself.

I have to bring everything to Annie.

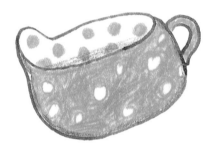

Today Annie is still a baby,
but Sparky is all grown up.

One day Annie will be big like Sparky and me.
But she'll always be my little sister.